Smokey's Great Escape

For anyone who has ever
wanted a kitten – SM

STRIPES PUBLISHING
An imprint of Magi Publications
1 The Coda Centre, 189 Munster Road,
London SW6 6AW

A paperback original
First published in Great Britain in 2010

Text copyright © Sue Mongredien, 2010
Illustrations copyright © Artful Doodlers, 2010
Photographs copyright © iStockphoto.com, 2010

ISBN: 978-1-84715-125-4

Sue Mongredien

Smokey's Great Escape

Meet the Kitten Club girls!

Amy
& Ginger

Mia
& Smokey

Molly
& Truffle

Ella
& Honey

Ruby
& Ziggy

Lily
& Buster

Chapter I

Ding-dong! At the sound of the doorbell, Mia Khaliq slid her sleeping kitten, Smokey, off her lap and on to the sofa, then jumped to her feet. It was Saturday afternoon, which meant only one thing – Kitten Club! The six members of the club were meeting at Mia's house, and she had been looking forward to seeing them again all week.

She eagerly pulled open the front door to see her friend Ella there. Mia knew Ella from school and riding lessons, but they had quite different personalities – Ella was something of a tomboy and liked playing football with the boys at break-time, whereas Mia preferred to chat or play imaginary games with her friends. But since they'd both got kittens, there was always *lots* to talk about!

"Hi again." Mia smiled. The two girls had already seen each other at their riding lesson that morning. "Come in. You're the first here." She was just closing the door when she saw a car pull up, and out scrambled Molly, Lily and Ruby.

Blonde-haired Lily waved excitedly, the Kitten Club scrapbook under her arm. "Hi, Mia!" she called up the drive.

Mia smiled. "Hi, Scatty," she replied,
calling Lily by her secret Kitten Club code
name. Lily was *very* loud, but great fun!
Forming the club had been Lily's idea, back
when the six girls had met whilst choosing
their kittens at Chestnut Farm. Dark-haired
Molly lived up the road from Lily – she was
very sporty and friendly – and Ruby was
Molly's best friend from school.

They hurried inside, and the hall was suddenly full of chatter. Then, as they were taking off their shoes, the doorbell rang again. "That must be Amy – I mean, Green-Eyes," Mia said, opening the door.

Amy was quite quiet compared to some of the other members of Kitten Club, but she had only recently moved to the area so was still finding her feet. She'd just started riding lessons with Mia and Ella that day, so Mia was hoping to get to know her a bit better.

"Hello," said Amy, smiling shyly.

"Hiya, come in," Mia said, and then let out a shriek as a fluffy grey streak shot past her ankles. "Smokey, come back!"

Smokey was a *very* lively kitten! He was always up to mischief and doing crazy things, and lately he'd seemed on a mission to escape the house. Whenever someone opened the front or back door, Smokey would be there within seconds, trying his hardest to get out and have an adventure in the big wide world!

Luckily, Amy reacted quickly and reached down to grab the cheeky kitten. "Gotcha!" she laughed, as Smokey squirmed in her hands. She stepped inside and Mia shut the door.

"Phew!" said Mia. "Sorry about that, Green-Eyes."

Lily giggled. "I think Mia was testing your kitten-catching skills before the meeting, Amy," she said. "And the good news is – you passed!"

"You totally passed," Mia agreed, gently taking her kitten from Amy. "Oh, Smokey! What am I going to do with you? You know you're not allowed out yet!"

"Honey is exactly the same," Ella said, as they went upstairs to Mia's bedroom. "She can't wait to get out and explore the garden, and hates the fact that Misty, our other cat, can go in and out of the magnetic cat flap. Poor Honey doesn't understand why it won't let her through. She keeps pushing against it with her head, meowing the saddest little meows."

"How does a magnetic cat flap work?"
Molly asked.

"Misty has a special magnet on her collar
that opens the door," Ella explained. "It's to
stop other cats coming into the house and
eating Misty's food – and it stops Honey
escaping too!"

"It won't be long until they can go
outside," Ruby put in. "Five weeks to go!"

"That's right, a week or so after their
second lot of vaccinations," Amy replied.

Mia opened her bedroom door – but her
heart sank when she saw Sunita was already in
there. Sunita was Mia's big sister and the two
of them shared a room. They got along most
of the time, but sometimes Sunita was really
bossy. And ever since Mia had got Smokey,
she'd seemed more bad-tempered than ever.

"This is my sister, Sunita," Mia said to the other girls. "Sunita, this is Lily, Ella, Ruby, Amy and Molly."

"Also known as Kitten Club!" Molly said with a friendly smile.

Sunita barely looked up from her book as she said hello, and Mia's face felt hot. She hoped Sunita wasn't going to be rude to her new friends.

Mia's side of the bedroom was rather

untidy as usual, so she passed Smokey to Ella to hold, then scooped up armfuls of clothes from her bed, and dumped them on the floor so that Amy, Ella and Molly could sit down. Then she cleared all the toys off her beanbag to make space for her and Ruby.

Lily was already stretched out on the floor, opening the Kitten Club scrapbook. She giggled as Smokey made a reckless dive off the bed and skidded on to the first page.

"Smokey's going to help me do the roll-call," said Lily. "Are you ready, Smokey? Here goes… Moggy?"

Molly, whose code name was Moggy, glanced over at Sunita. "Aren't the code names meant to stay secret?" she whispered.

Sunita raised an eyebrow. "Don't mind me," she said.

There was a moment's silence, then Lily tried again. "Moggy?"

"Meow," Molly replied, blushing as if she felt a bit silly.

"Glamour-Puss?"

"Meow!" said Ruby.

"Witch-Cat?"

"Meow!" said Mia.

There was a titter from Sunita on the other side of the room. "*Witch-Cat?*" she sniggered.

Mia frowned crossly. She wasn't going to have her sister spoiling the Kitten Club meeting by poking fun at them – no way! "Come on, guys," she said pointedly, getting to her feet and picking up Smokey. "Let's have our meeting in the garden instead. There's a bad smell in here."

"What, coming from you? Or your stinky kitten?" Sunita replied, but Mia was already striding out of the room, cheeks burning, with the other girls close behind.

Chapter 2

Down in the kitchen, the girls slipped on their shoes as Mia put Smokey in his basket, hoping he'd stay and play with his toys. But as soon as he saw the six friends heading towards the back door, he jumped out of the basket and followed them eagerly. "No, mister," Mia laughed, scooping him up. "You've got to stay in here."

She opened the back door to let the others out, returned Smokey to his basket, then dashed outside, shutting the door quickly behind her. *Phew!*

The girls sat down in the sunny garden and Lily opened up the scrapbook again. She ticked off Green-Eyes (Amy), Tomboy (Ella) and Scatty (herself), and then Kitten Club got down to business, with everyone writing their kitten's news into the book.

"Truffle is booked in for her first set of vaccinations next week," Molly said. "I can't believe she's nine weeks old already."

"Smokey's got his too," Mia said. "On Monday, poor thing."

"Ziggy's booked in on Monday as well," Ruby said, pulling a face. "I hope it won't hurt him. I don't think I'll be able to watch."

"It only hurts them for a moment," Ella said reassuringly. "And it will stop them getting horrible diseases that would be much more painful."

The back door opened just then, and Mia's little sister Aisha toddled outside. She was pushing a pink dolls' buggy, laden with a plastic tea-set. "You like tea?" she asked the Kitten Club girls, picking up a pink plastic teapot.

Mia leaped up to shut the back door before Smokey could escape. "Aisha, why don't you go and play with Mum?" she suggested. She really didn't want another sister spoiling the meeting.

But Aisha didn't seem to hear. She pushed the buggy over to the girls and began handing out tea-cups. "Tea!" she declared proudly.

Mia groaned. Sometimes she felt she never got a moment to herself, having two sisters! Thankfully the others didn't mind.

"Thank you," Ruby said gravely, pretending to sip from her cup. "Mmm, that's delicious!"

"She is so cute!" Amy said, smiling at Mia. "I wish I had a sister – or a brother!"

"No, you don't," said Molly, who had three older brothers.

"Talking of cute," Lily said, peering down to the end of the garden, "is that your rabbit, Mia?"

Everyone turned to look at the rabbit hutch. A fluffy white bunny was just lolloping through the door into its living

area, where it began nibbling the straw there. "That's Thumper, Sunita's rabbit," Mia explained. "She got him last year. Sweet, isn't he?"

"Really sweet," Ruby agreed, smiling.

"But not as sweet as our kittens! Whose turn is it to write in the book?"

"Mine," Lily said, taking the pen. "Buster's news this week is that he almost ended up in the washing machine! He fell asleep in the laundry basket, and Mum was just stuffing the dirty clothes into the machine when she heard a meow!"

Everyone laughed. "Honey had a surprise wash this week," Ella said, "although not in a washing machine. She managed to tip up her saucer of water and got completely soaked. She looked so cute, I took some photos – look!"

"Her fur looks like you've spiked it up with hair gel!" Molly said, giggling over the photos Ella passed around of poor soggy Honey. "She looks so skinny when she's all wet, doesn't she?"

After they'd exchanged all their news, the girls split into two teams and did a Kitten Quiz that Ella had cut out of a magazine the day before. Mia was on a team with Ruby and Amy, and they beat the others by a single point. Then they went back inside and played with Smokey, making him an obstacle course around the living room.

Before they knew it, their parents had arrived, and it was time to go home. "Shall we have our meeting at my house next Saturday?" Molly suggested.

"Great idea," Ruby said, and Molly scribbled down her address for the others.

"We'll have a lot to talk about," Ella pointed out, "what with the kittens' vaccinations, and school starting again on Monday."

"School! Oh, don't mention that word," Amy groaned. She hadn't been looking forward to beginning a new school, but at least she was going to the same one as Molly and Ruby.

"You'll be all right," Molly told her. "Me and Glamour-Puss will look after you."

Mia picked up Smokey and everyone gave him a last stroke.

"Thanks for having us," Lily said to Mia's mum, who'd come to see them out. "Bye Witch-Cat, bye Smokey, see you soon!"

"Bye Scatty," said Mia, making Smokey wave his little paw. She held on to him tightly as the front door opened and her friends trooped out with their parents. "No, you're not going with them," she laughed. "You're staying here with me, all right?"

Chapter 3

Mia woke with a start on Monday morning. "Mia!" her mum called, pulling open the bedroom curtains. "Come on, you'll be late for school if you don't get up now!"

Mia rubbed her eyes and looked at the time. Oh no! She'd managed to sleep right through Sunita's alarm clock. She struggled into her uniform and had to stuff her

breakfast down so fast she barely tasted it.
Sunita, of course, had been up for ages, and
was sitting with neatly plaited hair and her
school bags, all ready to go.

Mia only just remembered to give
Smokey some breakfast in her rush to brush
her hair and teeth. "I'm going to miss you
while I'm at school, Smokey," she said,
stroking him. "You be good while I'm gone,
won't you?"

"*I* look after him now," said Aisha. Mia
exchanged a worried glance with her mum.
She wasn't sure she liked the sound of that!

"We'll both look after Smokey," Mrs Khaliq said, giving Mia a reassuring smile.

Mia enjoyed seeing all her school friends again, but got told off twice in class by her new teacher, Mrs Andrews. First it was for daydreaming about Smokey. Then she was caught whispering to Ella about how Smokey had fallen asleep curled up in her bunny slipper the day before. Mrs Andrews fixed Mia with a beady eye and told her to get on with her work. Mia had a nasty feeling that Mrs Andrews was going to be a bit strict for her liking! She tried hard to get through the sums they'd been set, but her mind kept drifting to thoughts of Smokey.

Smokey had
been booked in
for his vaccinations
that afternoon and
Mia was dreading
it. She hoped he
would be OK.

As soon as
she got back
from school that
day, Mia had to
put Smokey in a
box with a lid, and then
she, her mum and sisters took him to the
vet. Mia's tummy felt more and more
churned up as she sat in the waiting room
with her mum and sisters. Smokey kept
walking around inside the box, which was

sitting on Mia's knee, meowing as if he felt anxious. "Don't worry," Mia said softly through the hole in the top of the box. "I'm here, it's OK."

It was noisy in the vet's. There were two dogs taking it in turns to bark and whine, a budgie cheeping in a cage, and a black cat in a cat-carrier that hissed every time one of the dogs looked its way. Mia was glad when it was finally their turn to be seen.

Inside the treatment room, the vet and his assistant made a big fuss of Smokey.

"Isn't he gorgeous?" cooed the assistant, whose name was Lisa. "What a poppet!"

"He's very sweet," agreed John the vet, carefully lifting Smokey out of the box. "A purr-fect specimen, you could say!"

John put Smokey on a table, where he

stared around at everything with wide, interested eyes.

"Good boy," Mia said, reaching out to ruffle his fur.

"I've got a rabbit called Thumper," Sunita put in. "She's *really* cute."

"That's nice," John said, keeping hold of Smokey. He turned to Mia's mum. "So, these vaccinations will protect Smokey from what we call 'the big three' – the really nasty viruses and illnesses that cats can get. I'll give him the first set today, and then you'll need to come back in three weeks for his booster injections."

Lisa handed John a syringe and Mia bit her lip, remembering having her own injections just before she'd started school – they had really hurt. Poor Smokey!

Mia couldn't bear the thought of that big needle being jabbed into his little body and looked away, hiding her face against her mum.

She heard a surprised meow from Smokey, and then, "All done," from John. She turned to see that Smokey had his ears back and was lashing his fluffy tail from side to side.

"Oh, Smokey," said Mia, giving him a cuddle. "Did that hurt? You were very brave."

"Thumper didn't make a fuss about his injections," Sunita commented.

"Smokey should be fine, but just keep an eye on him tonight," John advised. "And we'll see you in a few weeks' time."

John wrote out a special certificate to say that Smokey had had his first vaccinations, and gave it to Mia to look after. Then it was time to go. Just as they were leaving, they saw Ruby and her mum come in with a box.

"Is that Ziggy?" Mia said. "Smokey's just had his jabs. Don't worry, it's over really quickly," she added, seeing how nervous Ruby looked.

"Thanks," Ruby said, holding the box protectively. A meow came from inside, and then Smokey meowed from his box, as if he recognized his brother's voice!

Back at home, Mia got Smokey out to give him some tea, but he didn't seem at all himself. He didn't want any food, and he

didn't want to play either – he just curled up in his basket, looking rather sorry for himself. Mia felt worried. Was that normal? She phoned Ruby later that evening to see how Ziggy was doing.

"He's a bit quiet," Ruby said down the phone. "My brother wanted to play with him, but Ziggy got really cross and almost scratched him. Mum said it was probably best to let him sleep it off. I'm sure he and Smokey will both be fine tomorrow."

"Fingers crossed," Mia said, crossing hers tightly.

Thankfully, Ruby was right. The next morning when Mia went downstairs,

Smokey seemed much better, and was chomping his kitten food with gusto. Mia rushed over in relief … then stopped, as a thought struck her. "Mum, did you give Smokey his breakfast?" she asked.

Mia's mum was buttering some toast. "No, I think Sunita did," she replied, turning to Mia.

Mia glared at her sister who was stacking the dishwasher. "Sunita! Smokey's *my* kitten," she said crossly. "I can look after him myself!"

Sunita looked hurt. "I was only trying to be helpful," she muttered. "I won't bother next time."

She stalked out of the room, and Mia's mum gave Mia a reproachful look. "Mia, that wasn't very fair," she scolded. "Sunita was doing you a favour."

Mia sat down and began eating her cereal in silence. Sunita had her own pet, didn't she? Why did she have to interfere with Mia and her kitten?

Chapter 4

Mia had a busy week, as usual. There was gymnastics on Tuesday night, swimming on Wednesday, and Brownies on Thursday. She enjoyed going to all her clubs, but the only problem was that it meant less time with Smokey. Finally it was Friday, and Mia didn't have to do anything except go home and have a lovely long play with her kitten.

But as soon as she'd sat down with Smokey and his favourite squeaky mouse, her mum reminded her that Smokey's litter tray needed cleaning out.

"Oh, Mum! Can't I do it later?" Mia groaned. Cleaning out kitty litter was *gross*!

"*Now*, please," her mum replied crisply. "Come on, Mia, you've got to look after your pet responsibly. Sunita always cleans out Thumper's hutch without complaining."

Mia rolled her eyes as she went to get the bag of cat litter. Sometimes Sunita was irritatingly perfect!

"There," she said, once the tray had been emptied out and filled with fresh litter. "All done. And now it's time to play, Smokey!"

"Or you could do your homework first?" her mum suggested. "If you do it

now, you'll have the rest of the weekend
free to play."

Mia hesitated. Mrs Andrews had set
them a whole page of sums to do, and Mia
wasn't keen on maths at the best of times.
Smokey settled her dilemma by making a
flying leap on to Mia's foot and fighting
with a loose thread from her sock. Mia
giggled. The sums could wait. "I'll do my
homework tomorrow," she said. "Come on,
Smokey. Let's have some fun!"

On Saturday morning, Mia went riding
with Ella and Amy. And in the afternoon,
it was Kitten Club time again, this week at
Molly's house.

"Hello, Witch-Cat! Come in," said Molly,
when she answered the door.

"Hi, Moggy," Mia said, stepping inside.
She could hear a dog barking in the garden
as well as cheers and shouts of "Goal!"

She must have looked startled because
Molly laughed. "Welcome to the mad
house," she said cheerfully. "The others are
in the kitchen. This way!"

Mia followed Molly into a warm, sunny
kitchen, where Ruby, Lily, Ella and Amy
were already sitting around a large table.

Through the big windows, Mia could see three boys and a dog having a noisy game of football in the back garden. The boys had the same wavy hair as Molly, and even the same football tops.

Molly's tabby kitten Truffle was sitting on Ruby's knee and Mia went to stroke her. Truffle had beautiful stripy markings and long white whiskers, and she rumbled with purrs as Mia tickled her under the chin.

"Oh, you are so gorgeous." Mia smiled. "What a loud purr!"

After they'd done their usual roll-call, the girls got down to their kitten catch-up.

"Buster was quite poorly after his vaccinations," Lily said. "He went all droopy and feeble, it was horrible. He's much better now, thank goodness. I can't wait until he's had the second lot of jabs and can go outside. I've bought him the most gorgeous purple velvet collar."

"I've got Ginger a blue one," Amy said with a smile. "And guess what, the vet said Ginger looked very healthy when I took him to be vaccinated. I was a bit worried he might notice I'd been over-feeding him and tell me off, but I think Ginger must be down to his proper size now."

"That's good news," Mia said. She knew how upset Amy had been when the Kitten

Club girls had pointed out how tubby Ginger was looking a few weeks earlier. It turned out that Amy had been feeding him way too much, and all the wrong food! "How's Ziggy?" she asked Ruby.

"He's great – crazy, as usual!" Ruby replied. "But now that we're back at school, Mum says he's got to sleep downstairs. His bed was in my room before, but he kept waking me up, jumping on my hair and licking my face!" She giggled. "*I* didn't mind, but Mum said it was making me too tired for school. Poor Ziggy gets really upset about sleeping in the kitchen, though.

He's scratched the door really badly trying to get out!" She smiled at Mia. "How's Smokey been?"

"As mad as ever," Mia replied. "Still desperately trying to escape the house and explore – he's a total thrill-seeker. Roll on the last vaccinations so that he can finally go outside!"

"Yeah, and then we won't have to clean out yucky litter trays any more either," Lily put in, pulling a face. "Aren't they the worst thing in the world?"

"Even worse than brothers," Molly agreed with a grin.

Once everyone had written their news in the scrapbook, Molly produced a badge-making set she'd been given for her birthday, and they spent ages making Kitten

Club badges. Mia drew a grey
kitten in the middle of hers,
with a *K* and *C* in swirly writing
at the top.

"That is so cool, Mia," Amy
said admiringly. "I've tried to
draw Ginger but he looks
more like a little orange pig."

"And Ziggy looks cross-
eyed in my picture," Ruby
giggled. "I'd better not
show him – he'll be very offended!"

Everyone was having such fun, nobody
could believe it when the doorbell went,
and it was Amy's mum come to collect her.

"I love Kitten Club, but it always goes so
fast," Lily said with a theatrical sigh. "Why
can't school go as quickly? It's not fair!"

Chapter 5

The next day was Sunday, and as soon as Mia woke up, she padded downstairs to give Smokey his breakfast. When Smokey heard Mia rattling the box of kitten food, he bounded over at once and rubbed himself around Mia's ankles, purring.

"You *are* clever, Smokey," Mia said, tipping some food into Smokey's bowl and

mashing it up
with a bit of
water. Kittens
needed their
food moist when
they were as young
as Smokey. "You know
that rattling sound means something
yummy is on the way, don't you?"

Smokey purred even louder as he began
tucking in. Mia crouched next to him,
feeling very happy. She'd been looking
forward to today all week. For once, there
was nothing on the calendar, and she could
have a nice, lazy day at home with lots of
time spent playing with Smokey.

But her mum had other ideas. "Mia, could
you take the rubbish out for me?" she asked,

heaving a full black bag out of the kitchen bin and tying it at the top. "And after that, you need to tidy your bedroom. Your side of the room is an absolute tip – you can hardly see the carpet around your bed, there's so much stuff on the floor."

Mia sighed. Chores! Tidying! This wasn't how she wanted to spend her Sunday! But she got up, put on her shoes, and lugged the bin bag over to the back door. Gosh, it was heavy! She struggled to open the back door one-handed and then, just as she managed it, Smokey seized the chance to make a break for freedom and shot past her ankles.

"Oh, Smokey!" Mia cried, dumping the rubbish bag and chasing after him. She grabbed him just as he was about to disappear under a shrub, then took him up to her room and shut the door. "You stay there and start tidying while I put the rubbish out. I'll be right back!" she told him.

Once she'd dumped the heavy bin bag into the dustbin, she washed her hands and went back upstairs to her room. Her mum was right – her side was a real mess, with a jumble of clothes, art stuff, toys and books scattered all over the place. Of course, Sunita's side of the room was spotless, with everything neatly put away in her drawers.

Smokey poked his head out of a big pile of clothes and meowed happily at Mia, before pouncing on the zip of her Brownie

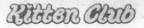

hoodie and rolling on to his
side with it between his
tiny paws. Then he
vanished completely
under the pink
top Mia had
been wearing
the day before.

Mia couldn't help laughing. "Are you
exploring, Smokey?" she said. "Don't get
lost under there, will you?"

She lay on her tummy and forgot all about
tidying up as she played with Smokey.
Smokey loved chasing Mia's red glittery belt
when it was dragged along in front of him,
and was fascinated by one of Mia's pens that
had blue feathers glued to its end. He stared
at it, wild-eyed, then hunched low, wiggled his

bottom in the air and pounced. Mia burst into giggles. "Did you think that was a strange blue bird?" she said, as Smokey wrestled with the pen. "Oh, Smokey!"

Sunita came in a while later to put away some books she'd been using for her homework, and even she laughed at the sight of Smokey chasing marbles all around the room like a miniature footballer. "You're nearly as good as Molly and Ella," Mia giggled.

"He's so cute," Sunita said, smiling, and Mia smiled back. For the first time in ages, she felt warm towards her big sister – but just then, the door opened and in came their mum.

"Mia! This room looks worse than ever!" she scolded. Then she caught sight

of Smokey tearing out from under Mia's bed, still in pursuit of a big blue marble. "Oh, so *that's* why you haven't started tidying. Well, I think it's time Smokey went downstairs, while you get on with clearing up this mess." She bent down and scooped up Smokey, who didn't look at all happy to have his game of football interrupted.

Sunita followed their mum – and Smokey – downstairs. "I'll take him, Mum," Mia heard Sunita say. "I've finished all my homework now."

Mia gave a sigh. Sometimes she secretly wished she could be as organized as her big sister. Still, the sooner she could clear everything up, the sooner she could get back to playing with Smokey. That was one good reason to get stuck in, wasn't it?

Later on, when everything had been picked up and put away (or shoved under the bed out of sight), Mia hurried back downstairs in search of Smokey. She had the marbles and her feathery pen tucked in her jeans pocket ready for another game. But when she went into the living room, she found that Smokey was already playing with Sunita.

"Come and get it!" Sunita giggled, pulling a piece of string along the carpet. Sunita had tied a scrunched-up piece of paper to the string, and Smokey was having a wonderful time chasing after it.

Mia felt a stab of jealousy. "Hey, Smokey, look what I've got!" she said, rolling the marble towards him. But Smokey

didn't seem to notice Mia was even there.
He went on scampering after Sunita's
home-made toy, chasing and pouncing
on it.

Mia tried again, tickling Smokey with the
feathery end of her pen. "What's this,
then?" she asked, brushing the feathers over
Smokey's soft fur. But Smokey was so busy
chewing Sunita's toy that he paid the
feathers no attention whatsoever.

Sunita grinned. "He likes me best," she teased.

"No he doesn't!" Mia replied hotly. "He's *my* kitten, remember!"

Their dad was sitting on the sofa reading a newspaper. He looked up when he heard Mia's cross voice. "Mia, that's enough," he said sternly. "Smokey *is* your kitten, but everyone can play with him."

"Yes, but—" Mia protested.

"No buts," her dad interrupted. "Now, I believe you've got some homework to do, haven't you? Bring it in here, and I'll have a look at it with you."

"Oh, Dad…" Mia said. Tidying up, homework – this was not how she wanted her Sunday to be!

"Come on, Mia," her dad said. "It won't take long. There'll be plenty of time for playing once you've finished."

Mia opened her mouth to argue, but she could tell from the look on her dad's face that he wasn't about to back down. Gritting her teeth, she went to get her homework book, with Sunita's giggles ringing in her ears.

Chapter 6

On Monday, Mia had a nice surprise. She'd been learning to play the violin in school for a while now, and when she had a lesson that day, her teacher, Mr Amies, told her he thought she was good enough to join the school orchestra. "We meet every Friday after school," Mr Amies said, giving her a letter to take home to her parents with all

the details on. "It would be great to have you with us, Mia."

Mia was delighted. The school orchestra was really good – they put on a big Christmas concert for the parents every year, and Mia loved the thought of taking part.

As soon as school finished that day, she ran over to where her mum and Aisha were waiting by the school gates. "Mum, look," she burst out. "I've been chosen for the orchestra!" She rummaged in her book bag to find the letter, and thrust it into her mum's hands.

Mrs Khaliq's mouth twisted uncertainly as she read the letter. "Well… Let's talk about this at home," she said after a moment. For some reason, she didn't look as pleased as Mia had hoped.

"Talk about what?" Sunita asked, joining them.

"Orchestra," Mia replied, hopping from foot to foot. "I'm going to be in the school orchestra!"

Sunita wrinkled her nose as if she thought that was boring, but Mia didn't care. Sunita might be great at school work and being tidy and perfect, but she didn't have a musical bone in her body. For once, Mia had been picked for something that Sunita wasn't already best at. It made Mia feel really special.

She daydreamed about it all the way home, imagining standing on stage, playing her violin in front of all the other parents. What if Mr Amies gave her a solo? How exciting it would be! She got goosebumps all over at the thought.

But later that evening, when Mia's dad was home, it became clear that her parents weren't so sure that she should join another club. "We think you've got enough on already," her dad said gently. "What with Brownies, swimming, gymnastics, riding *and* Kitten Club, that's plenty for anyone. There's homework too, of course, and you've got Smokey now as well. You need time to look after him, don't you?"

Mia was dismayed. "But I *really* want to join the orchestra," she protested. "Please?"

Her mum shook her head. "I'm sorry, love," she said. "But I've had to clean out Smokey's litter tray and food bowls a lot since we've had him, when that was something you agreed to do. And you haven't been keeping your room tidy lately either. If you join the orchestra as well, you'll have even less time to look after Smokey and do your chores."

"I'll make time – I promise!" Mia said.

"No, Mia," her dad said. "It's a no, and that's our final word on the subject."

"What's up, Mia?"

Mia looked up at the sound of Ella's voice. It was the next day at school, and she still felt upset at her parents' decision. She'd barely been able to concentrate on anything Mrs Andrews had said that morning. Now it was playtime, and she didn't feel like joining in with her friends. She gave Ella a small smile and told her what had happened.

Ella sat next to her on the bench. "That's a shame," she said. "Are you sure they won't change their minds?"

"Very sure," Mia replied sadly. "It's so unfair. They let *Sunita* do loads of clubs when she's got a pet too." She felt thoroughly sorry for herself. "Just because she's super-organized, she gets to do everything she wants!"

"Well, maybe that's it," Ella said thoughtfully. "Maybe *you* need to be a bit more organized."

"Mmmm," Mia agreed, although she couldn't help but feel doubtful. For someone who was always getting told off for being messy or lost in a daydream, she wasn't sure being organized was possible.

"You just need to show your mum and dad you can do it," Ella went on. "Maybe you could draw up a chart where you write down all your chores, plus things you have

to do for Smokey – feeding him, brushing him, cleaning out the litter tray – and then you can tick things off when you've done them. That way you won't forget, and you'll be able to keep on top of everything."

"That's a really good idea," Mia replied. "You're a genius, Ella! Mum and Dad will see that I'm serious about getting everything done – and I'll actually remember to do it all!"

"Come on," Ella said, jumping off the wall.

"Where are we going?" Mia asked, following her friend.

"To find somewhere to sit and draw up your chart, of course," Ella replied with a grin. "The new, improved, super-organized Mia Khaliq starts right here!"

Chapter 7

Thanks to Ella's brilliant plan, Mia felt very efficient during the next few days. She and Ella had made a grid that had the days of the week running down one side, then the things she had to do in columns across the top. There were boxes to tick whenever she fed, groomed and played with Smokey, boxes for when she'd cleaned his food bowls

and changed the cat litter, and extra boxes
for homework, learning her spellings, violin
practice and tidying her bedroom.

Mia had stuck the chart up in the kitchen
so that her parents could see it, and loved
ticking things off every day. So far, it was
going brilliantly – and her parents had
noticed.

"This was such a good idea,
Mia," her dad said warmly,
as she ticked off her
'Spellings' box on
Thursday. "We're
really impressed
that you're doing so
well. Keep it up!"

Mia glowed
with pride.

Being organized wasn't so hard after all. Just a few more days of the new routine and she would ask her parents about the school orchestra again. Hopefully they would agree that she *could* take on another activity without a problem!

But when Mia came back from school on Thursday afternoon, she found her chart ruined. Naughty Aisha had scribbled all over it, as well as on the kitchen wall.

"I'm sorry, Mia," her mum said. "I was in the garden for five minutes, hanging out the washing, and must have left the felt-tips on the table. I'll make you another chart tomorrow, OK?"

Mia couldn't help feeling annoyed with her sister. If it wasn't Sunita, it was Aisha spoiling things for her!

The next morning started badly. After a late
night at Brownies, Mia overslept by twenty
minutes and felt so tired and groggy she
couldn't think straight. It wasn't until they
were halfway to school that Sunita said
casually, "I hope Smokey isn't going to be
too hungry today."

Mia frowned – and then her stomach
flipped in horror. In her mad scramble to
get ready for school, she'd completely
forgotten to give Smokey any breakfast!

"Oh no!" she cried in dismay. "Poor
Smokey!" She felt absolutely awful that
she'd forgotten.

"Oh, Mia," her mum said crossly.
"That's really not good enough. I can feed

him when I get home from dropping you off, but you should have remembered."

"I'm sorry, Mum, but without my chart, I just forgot, and…" Mia rounded on her big sister. "You could have reminded me, Sunita!"

Sunita held up her hands, all innocent. "Me? Last time I tried to help you by giving Smokey his breakfast, you shouted at me, remember? Why would I want to help you again?"

Mia felt like crying. She'd tried so hard to be organized this week, but everything had gone wrong now. Poor Smokey would be starving – and her parents would never change their minds about letting her join the school orchestra!

Thank goodness Ella was coming to tea after school and she had *something* nice to look forward to.

Mia felt much better as they walked home from school together, with her mum and sisters. It was Friday afternoon, and the start of the weekend – which meant Kitten Club!

"I can't wait to see Smokey again," Ella said, linking her arm through Mia's as they walked along.

Aisha, who was being wheeled along in the buggy, overheard. "I look after Smokey," she said importantly.

"Thanks, Aisha, but I think I can manage," Mia replied, pulling a funny face at Ella.

"Apart from giving him breakfast, that is," Sunita muttered.

Mia pretended to ignore her, and walked a little faster. She was *not* going to let Sunita get to her any more today!

Once they were home, Mia took Ella through to the kitchen, expecting to see Smokey there as usual. Her parents had thought it a good idea to restrict Smokey to a couple of rooms while he was little, so that he could always find his litter tray, and didn't get lost in the house. Usually, Smokey was shut in the kitchen when everyone else was out … but today he was nowhere to be seen.

"I bet he's hiding somewhere, the cheeky thing," Mia said. She picked up the box of kitten food and rattled it. That would have Smokey bounding out from his hiding place, she was certain of it! But Smokey didn't appear.

"That's weird," Mia said, puzzled. Her heart began to beat faster. "Mum, where's Smokey?"

Her mum looked surprised. "Isn't he in his basket?" she said. "He was in here earlier, I'm sure."

Mia turned to her little sister. "Aisha, do you know where Smokey is?"

Aisha nodded earnestly. "I look after him," she said again.

Mia was starting to feel panicky. Why did Aisha keep saying that? "Where is he?" she asked.

"He go out," Aisha replied, pointing at the back door. "He want go out. I let him!" She beamed, clearly thinking this was a good thing to have done.

Mia gasped. "You let him go *outside*?"

Aisha nodded proudly. "He play in garden." She beamed. "Aisha like garden – Smokey like garden!"

75

Mia couldn't speak, she felt so sick with worry. Smokey was way too young to be allowed out! He hadn't had his second set of vaccinations, he didn't have a collar or identity tag – and he might have got round the front of the house to the road! "Oh no!" she cried, yanking the back door open. "Come on, we've got to find him!"

Chapter 8

She and Ella hurtled outside. "Smokey!
Smokey! Come here, boy!" Mia yelled at the
top of her voice. Her heart thumped. She
couldn't believe this was happening.
"SMOKEY!"

Sunita was suddenly next to her, a hand
on her arm. "Don't shout so loud, you
might scare him," she said.

Mia was all set to shout at *her* for interfering, but Sunita spoke first. "Calm down and let's think where he might have gone," she said. "He probably won't have climbed over the back fence, it's too high. Maybe he's scrambled through to one of the gardens next door. I'll start going round the neighbours, asking if anyone has seen him."

Mia gaped at the cool way Sunita was tackling this disaster. "Thanks," she managed to say, as Sunita hurried back inside. Her sister was right, she had to try to stay calm.

She peered through the hedge that separated their garden from Mrs Lilley's on the left. "Smokey! Are you there? Smokey, it's me, Mia!"

"Din-dins, Smokey, din-dins!" Ella called. She caught Mia looking at her and blushed. "Sorry, that's what I say to Honey when I'm calling her for her food."

A lightbulb went on in Mia's head. *Food!* Smokey always came when Mia rattled the box of kitten food, didn't he? "That's it!" she cried. "I'll be right back." And she rushed into the house to fetch the box.

Back in the garden, Mia shook the box
of kitten food as if it were a tambourine.
"Smokey! Tea-time! Smokey!" she called,
again and again. "Smokey!"

Sunita appeared a few minutes later, her cheeks pink where she'd been running. "Mrs Jackson at number forty-four thinks she saw him earlier," she said. "She thought it was odd that such a tiny kitten could be out on his own and tried to catch him, but Smokey gave her the slip and ran into number forty-six. I've tried knocking, but there's no reply. Mum's writing a note to put under their door."

Mia bit her lip, feeling more worried than ever. Their house was number forty, and the thought of Smokey scampering through all those other gardens to number forty-six was awful. Where had he got to now? Would he even be able to hear them?

"Well, we know he went that way at least," Sunita said, pointing to the right. "Smokey!"

"Smokey!" called Mia, a sob in her voice. "Please come back. Smokey!" Maybe Smokey had run away because she had forgotten to feed him that morning, Mia thought miserably. Maybe Smokey had gone to look for a nicer home, one where his owner had more time for him!

The girls called and called, and Mia kept shaking the box of kitten food for what seemed like ages. Mia's mum and Aisha came out to help too, but still there was no sign of Smokey's dear little fluffy face.

Then, just as Mia was starting to lose hope, there came a rustling sound in the hedge to their right. Mia stopped shouting and held her breath as through the leaves, looking very bedraggled and wild, came Smokey.

As soon as he saw Mia, he rushed
straight up to her, purring loudly. His ears
were back, his tail was fluffed up like a
bottle brush and there were bits of leaves in
his fur. Clearly wherever he'd been, he'd had
a BIG adventure!

"Oh, Smokey!" Mia wanted to cry as she
picked him up and cuddled him close. "Oh,
I'm so glad to see you again! Where have
you been?"

"Thank goodness
he's all right!" said
Mia's mum, as Mia
and Ella fussed over
him. "Let's all go back
in, shall we? And we'll
keep that door *shut*!"

In they went, and Mia took Smokey
straight to his feeding mat and gave him
some of the kitten food, mashing it up just
the way he liked it. Smokey gobbled up the
food eagerly, obviously hungry after all his
exploring.

"Mia, I'm really sorry," her mum said.
"I should never have left Aisha alone with
Smokey – this is my fault."

"I sorry too," Aisha said, her big brown
eyes brimming with tears. "I naughty."

Mia's heart melted and she gave her sister a hug. "You're not naughty," she said. "I know you thought you were being kind, letting Smokey out. You won't do it again, though, will you?"

Aisha shook her head firmly. "Not do it again," she agreed. Then she produced her pink plastic teapot. "Cup of tea?" she asked hopefully.

Mia and Ella looked at each other and burst out laughing. "I'd love one," Mia told her sister.

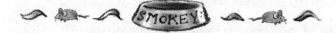

"So that's what Smokey has been up to – a big adventure in the great outdoors," Mia finished. It was Saturday afternoon, and she was round at Ruby's house, where this week's Kitten Club get-together was taking place. Everyone was wearing their new club badges, and the girls were taking it in turns to tell the others their kitten news. Mia had a lot to report, of course!

"Whoa!" Lily gasped, stroking Ruby's kitten Ziggy, who was on her lap. "You must have been so freaked out when you realized he'd gone outside!"

"I was," Mia replied. "Scared, mad with Aisha, guilty because I'd forgotten to feed him that morning..." She rolled her eyes.

"I was so glad to see him again when he came wriggling through the hedge."

"Oh, Mia, it sounds awful!" Ruby said.

"It was," Mia replied. "But some good things have come out of it. Last night, after you'd gone home, Tomboy, I had a heart-to-heart with Sunita. We haven't been getting on well lately, but now I know why. She told me she'd been feeling jealous of me having

Smokey, because he's much more fun than
Thumper is, and that was why she'd been
acting strangely. She even said she was
jealous of Kitten Club."

"What did you say to that?" Amy asked.

Mia grinned. "I suggested she starts a
Rabbit Club with some of her friends. And
do you know what? She said she might just
do that!"

"Good thinking!" Molly laughed, then touched her badge where she'd pinned it on her top. "Although they'll have to try really hard to make their badges cooler than ours!"

Mia smiled to herself. It had actually been really nice having a proper chat with Sunita again. Mia had even admitted to feeling a bit jealous herself, when she'd seen Sunita playing with Smokey the weekend before. "I was worried he liked you more than me," she'd confessed.

"No way," Sunita had replied. "Smokey is your kitten, and he loves you best. Definitely!" She'd smiled. "Maybe he likes me second best, though."

And that, thought Mia, was fine by her.

"What happened yesterday did really

make me think," she went on now to her friends. "It made me realize just how important Smokey is to me. He is number one on my list, not gym or riding, or even trying to persuade my parents to let me join the orchestra."

Ella turned to her in surprise. "What — so you're giving up on the orchestra, then?" she asked.

Mia nodded. "I am," she said. Then she wrinkled her nose. "Well, not giving up *totally*," she replied. "I'm still having violin lessons at school, and Mum says I can join the orchestra next term if I drop one of my other clubs. I figured the orchestra could wait, but Smokey is only going to be a kitten once. I want to make the most of my time with him." She grinned. "And in the meantime, Mum's helped me make a new chart that we've put up out of Aisha's reach, so that I can keep myself a bit more organized."

"Good for you, Witch-Cat," Amy said, tickling Ziggy, who'd jumped off Lily's lap and was now playing with the frayed threads at the bottom of Amy's jeans. "You kittens are too good to miss out on, aren't you?"

Meow went Ziggy, as if he understood every word.

Mia smiled. "It's true," she said. "Having a kitten is the most lovely thing in the world. All the cuddling, all the playing, all the purring…"

"And best of all, having brilliant Kitten Club friends," Lily put in, her eyes twinkling. "Yay for Kitten Club!"

Have you read...

Sue Mongredien

Kitten Club

Ginger's New Home

Coming soon...

Sue Mongredien

Kitten Club

Ziggy's Midnight Feast

To find out more about the author, visit:
www.suemongredien.co.uk